OVER
THE LINE

TOM PALMER

With illustrations by
Ollie Cuthbertson

Conkers

First published in 2014 in Great Britain by
Barrington Stoke Ltd
18 Walker Street, Edinburgh, EH3 7LP

www.barringtonstoke.co.uk

This edition first published in 2020

Text © 2014 Tom Palmer
Illustrations © 2014 Ollie Cuthbertson

A CIP catalogue record for this book is available
from the British Library upon request

ISBN: 978-1-78112-956-2

Printed and bound by CPI Group (UK) Ltd, Croydon, CR0 4YY

For Jack

Do people ever ask what you want to be when you grow up?

What do you say to them?

That you'd like to be a doctor? A singer? A soldier? A vet?

Or do you say, "I want to be a footballer"?

That was my dream when I was a boy. To be a footballer. To play for my country.

And, for me, the dream came true.

Sort of.

So, now I am waiting for the whistle. When that whistle blows, my dream to play for my country will come true. I will go over the line.

But I never dreamed it would be like this.

PART 1
Footballer

ONE

It was the day of my debut as a professional footballer. My dream had come true.

But even when your dream comes true, you still have to keep trying.

Within a minute of kick-off, Fred Bullock passed the ball to me. He was my team captain at Huddersfield Town. I controlled the ball with my left foot, then played it wide to our winger. So far, so good.

Now it was my duty to get into the penalty area. I was a forward. I was a goal scorer. Our winger would cross the ball soon, so I needed to get up field.

The mud was thick on the pitch, even though the game had only just begun.

A Grimsby defender tracked me as I powered towards the goal. Sid Wheelhouse. His deep-furrowed frown made him look like a bull and he was big too. Big and strong.

The ball came in from the left.

I strained every muscle to reach it.

I lunged towards the Grimsby keeper. But somehow Wheelhouse had come between us. I hit him hard, but I just bounced off him and the keeper collected the ball close to his chest.

No goal. Not a sniff of a goal. And I wanted one.

The first half of that first game was tough. I didn't get past Wheelhouse once. He tracked my runs. He beat me to the ball. He protected his goalkeeper.

When the referee blew the whistle for half-time, I put my hands on my knees.

All that effort and nothing to show for it. I felt a fierce frustration deep inside – a sense of panic that things weren't going to plan. I had to do better in the second half.

Or this could end up being my last game as a professional footballer, as well as my first.

I followed my team-mates off the pitch, the sweat on my body cooling now I had stopped running.

Fred Bullock came up to me and gave me a powerful slap on the back. He pushed back his dark hair and smiled. "You worked hard," he said. "You got into the right places. Keep doing what you're doing."

I nodded, still too breathless to talk. But I was pleased. Perhaps I hadn't been as bad as I thought.

As we walked off the pitch, I saw a group of people gathered by the players' tunnel. They were shouting and waving wooden signs.

"Who are they?" I asked Bullock.

"Protesters," he replied.

"Protesters?" I said. "Against what?"

"Against footballers," he said. "You and me. They're angry that we're playing football instead of fighting."

He meant fighting in France, as soldiers. The year was 1914 and our country was at war. The Germans had invaded Belgium and France and the British Army was over there fighting them. Tens of thousands of men had volunteered to join up.

"That bald man is an MP," Bullock went on. "He thinks there should be a battalion of football players."

I looked at the protesters as we passed. I understood why they wanted men to fight – young men like me. But this was my debut as a professional footballer. Why should a war come between me and my big chance? A war that would be over in weeks.

Then a woman stepped out of the crowd and reached out to give me something. Her hand was so cold that it shocked me. I took what she had given me, but I kept walking.

"Who was that woman?" I asked Bullock as we walked down the tunnel.

"Roebuck's wife," he said.

Larrett Roebuck was a Huddersfield Town player who had been killed by the Germans two months before. I had put some money into a fund for his family when he died.

And now Roebuck's wife had given me a piece of paper torn from a magazine. Bullock and I looked at it together. It was a cartoon. A character called Mr Punch was talking to a footballer at the side of the pitch. "No doubt you can make money on the football field," it said, "but there's only one field where you can get honour."

"What does it mean?" I asked Bullock.

Bullock paused. Then he asked, "You're making money playing football today?"

"Yes, of course," I said. "It's my job. I get paid."

"The cartoon is asking if you get honour from it too," Bullock explained. "As well as money."

"Honour?" I asked. "Like I would get if I was fighting?"

"That's it," Bullock said. His face was serious. "That question is for you and me. How can we play on a football field, when men like Roebuck are dying

in France on the field of war? We need to go too. That's the honourable thing to do."

I nodded. I understood now.

I also understood that Sid Wheelhouse was not the biggest threat to my football career. The biggest threat was the war.

"But forget that for now, Jack," Bullock said. "You need your mind on today's game, right?"

TWO

The second half had just started when the protesters spilled onto the pitch. They were louder now, and their voices echoed around the ground. Others had come down from the terraces to join in, inspired by the speeches at half-time.

It was hard to focus on the game – for me and for everyone.

The referee stopped the game and the protesters began to sing. First a few voices, then more.

"*Onward Christian soldiers,*
marching as to war ..."

I stood and listened, close to the centre circle, stretching my legs to keep my muscles warm.

"It's not going to go away," a voice behind me said.

I looked round to see Sid Wheelhouse, the defender who had given me nothing all game. He was standing with Summers, the young Grimsby keeper.

I nodded. Wheelhouse was right. These people were not going anywhere, and nor was the war. My dream had only just come true, and now it was crumbling.

"Is that Larrett Roebuck's widow?" Wheelhouse asked.

"It is," I said.

Wheelhouse shook his head. "I heard Roebuck was ex-army," he said. "They called him up on the day they declared war."

I nodded again, and then we stood in silence and looked at the protesters. They were singing louder now.

"Did you hear that bald MP going on about the Footballers' Battalion at half-time?" Wheelhouse asked me, after a few minutes had passed.

"What battalion?" Summers asked. He was a thin lad, with curly hair and a high-pitched voice. He looked more like a boy than a man, especially next to Wheelhouse.

"The Footballers' Battalion," Wheelhouse told him. "It was set up last month. There's an artists' battalion. A musicians' battalion. And now there's one for us."

Summers looked panicked as he turned to me. "Do you think you'll do it?" he asked.

"What?" I said. "Sign up?"

"Yes."

I shook my head.

"So, you don't care about the things people are saying about footballers, then?" Wheelhouse said.

"What are they saying?" I asked.

"They say we're not fit to fight. They say we're just interested in making money from football. Rugby players are fighting. Cricketers are fighting. But not footballers. They say we're too scared of being shot at and bombed."

"Lots of footballers have gone to fight," I said, annoyed. "Roebuck went."

"He did," Wheelhouse said. "But he was called up. I'm talking about volunteers. People will keep saying those things until footballers start to volunteer."

I felt uncomfortable. I hated it when people said bad things about football.

"What about you?" I asked Wheelhouse.

"I'm going to volunteer," he said.

I looked at Wheelhouse. I could imagine him on the battlefield. He was hard as nails. Nothing would stop him.

"You can't volunteer," Summers said. "You've got kids, a wife. What if ..."

"What if I end up dead like Larrett Roebuck?" Wheelhouse said, with a bitter laugh. "What if my wife ends up like that poor cow?"

Summers stared at his feet, at a loss as to what to say.

"I know a bloke whose wife and kids were killed in Scarborough, mate," Wheelhouse said. "The Germans are attacking us here. Next time it could be my wife and my children. Unless we stop them."

I'd read about that in the newspaper. At the start of December the war had come to Britain. Four German ships had bombarded Scarborough,

Hartlepool and Whitby. They came out of the sea one night and killed dozens of people in their beds. Hundreds more were hurt. And all less than a hundred miles from where we stood.

Summers and I stayed quiet.

Then the referee blew his whistle to restart the game. The sound left Wheelhouse's words hanging in the air with the fog gathering above the ground as night closed in.

I knew I had to focus on the football when Fred Bullock came up alongside me five minutes after the restart. He shoved me and caught my eye with a sharp glare.

"Mind on the game, Jack," he said.

So I cleared my mind of the war and of Roebuck's widow, and I focused on the match.

I ran harder. I tackled harder. I put everything in.

How could I have forgotten that this was my first-team debut? How could I have forgotten that today was the day that everything I wanted in life was within my grasp? I had to play like this was my last game. I had to get everything out of it that I could.

And then, because I was putting my heart into it, because I was working hard, my moment came. I got the ball in the midfield and shielded it, then played it out to the wing. Now I had to get onto the other side of Wheelhouse. Again.

I used all the power I could find in my legs to force myself past him. As I passed, I sensed that he had slowed down. Older players lose their pace later in the game – everyone knows that. And then there was the mud.

The mud gave me space.

Summers was rooted to his goal line, hesitating. That gave me the few seconds I needed as the ball came in low and hard. I lunged at it, and caught it with the side of my right boot. Then I lost my balance and fell.

The noise of the crowd told me that I had scored. Thousands of Yorkshiremen cheering. Then Fred Bullock's hand came down to haul me out of the mud. I saw blood streaming from his elbow to his hand as he pulled me up.

"Well taken, Jack," he said.

And that was it. I was a professional footballer. I had scored a goal. It felt so good that I didn't even see the protesters as I walked off the pitch at the end of the game.

THREE

Two weeks later, I played my second match for Huddersfield Town. It was a fine afternoon. I scored the winner from six yards – a header. But then the game was over and there were more protesters. This time they were giving out printed leaflets.

I took one and read it. It said that no young unmarried men should be in England. They should all be fighting in France.

Bullock's wife had invited me to their home to eat that night. I was only 19 and away from my parents for the first time, and she knew that I would need a good meal. I said "yes" to her invitation without hesitating. I was glad she wanted to look after me, not pack me off to war.

Bullock and I walked through the streets of Huddersfield in a heavy fog. It reminded me of autumn nights at home, when the mist came off the river. It made me miss my parents.

"You did well again, Jack," Bullock said.

"Thank you," I said.

The icy track under our feet felt solid. I asked myself if it was this cold in France where men were dug into trenches. Colder, probably, since they were out in the countryside.

Bullock stopped on the corner of a street of terraced houses.

"Before we go in," he said, "there's something I have to tell you."

I knew what was coming.

"I've decided to enlist," he said. "I'm going down to London on Monday to sign my papers."

"When did you decide?" I asked. I tried to keep my voice calm, but I had a terrible feeling that it should be me joining up, not him. The feeling was something like shame, with a bit of panic thrown in. In the end, I couldn't keep it in.

"It shouldn't be you," I said. "It's me who should—"

Bullock interrupted. "You don't need to explain yourself," he said. "Your decision is for you. I've talked it through with the wife and she agrees. After the Germans started bombing the coast and London, well ..."

"You've got children," I said. "I'm single. No children."

"You've just started your career," Bullock said. "And my family is the reason I need to fight. The war is in Britain now – I need to protect them."

22

Bullock stepped away and pushed open his front door. Two children came at him like a pair of dogs. One grabbed his legs while the other ran and jumped for his chest. A third child reached out from her mother's arms. She was no more than six months old. They all shouted and squealed until they saw me standing behind Fred on the cold pavement.

Then they stepped back, silent.

"Children," Fred said, "meet Jack. Jack is going to play football for England one day."

I tried to smile. Bullock knew I was determined to play for my country. But my thoughts were confused. Football. The war. Everything. Fred had given me an excuse not to join up. But should I give up on my dream of a professional football career?

FOUR

Highbury Stadium in north London took my breath away. It was more like a palace than a football ground. The glass and stone entrance and marble halls made it even more impressive than Stamford Bridge, where I used to go to watch Chelsea.

I'd played several games for Huddersfield by the time we played Arsenal. My performances had got better as I became happier among my team-mates. But I was nervous about this game. We were in the capital, playing one of the best teams around.

We came from the railway station on a coach, and we saw London at war. Soldiers marched through the streets. Horses pulled huge guns to the docks, bound for France.

I was trying to put the war out of my mind, to focus only on football. But the meaning of the name of the other team – Arsenal – was not lost on me.

Arsenal was a team born of war. An arsenal is a place where the weapons of war are stored, and Arsenal Football Club drew its first players from the Woolwich Arsenal in London. That was where they made the bombs and guns and bullets that were being used right now in the trenches in France.

When I followed my team-mates into the stadium, I could smell cigar smoke. It reminded me of my dad. He had one cigar a year, at Christmas, as a treat. But here people had the money to smoke cigars every day. They wore smarter clothes as well. There were dozens of men in fine suits and hats and coats. They made me feel very nervous. I began to feel that this place was too good for the likes of me.

And then Bullock stopped dead in front of me.

I put my hand on his shoulder to stop myself from banging into him. "What is it?" I asked.

"Norris," Bullock said. "Henry Norris. Owns Arsenal. Runs the Footballers' Battalion. Look out for him, he's dangerous."

I looked and saw a short, stocky man standing there, looking back at us. He had a pink face and a wiry white moustache.

"I will," I said, feeling twice as nervous now. This big fancy stadium and its important people had got to me. I wasn't sure I could play my best.

The Huddersfield Town team were lined up in the dressing room and ready to go out onto the pitch when Norris burst in.

"Good afternoon, gentlemen," he said.

Most of our players knew who Norris was. Some of them muttered "hello" or "good afternoon". As

he eyed us, the sharp smell of his cologne filled the room.

Then we waited. This was his stadium.

"At ease, gentlemen," Norris said at last. "I came to wish you luck. This is a big stage for a small-town team. But we're happy to welcome you here."

I could see that our gaffer was cross. This was the time for him to fire us up, get us right in the head for the match. Now this puffed-up man with his white moustache and beady eyes was doing the opposite.

"Most of my lads have already signed the form," Norris said. "Off to fight the Germans. And I'm proud of them. They're patriots." He paused. "I know this is a big day for you, this game against the Arsenal, but I still want you to think about enlisting. You're footballers – fit, strong men! You should be going out to fight."

We were all wise to what Norris was doing. He was trying to make us worry about the war, instead of focusing on the next 90 minutes. But none of us could stop him. We just listened, while a smile crept across his face. I could barely think about the game now. My head had gone.

When Norris left, the gaffer stepped to the front and stood on the exact spot where Norris had been. He looked each of us in the eye, one by one. He stopped at me.

"Who are we, Jack?" he asked.

"What?" I had no idea what he meant, or why he had picked me.

"Who are we?" he demanded. "What team?"

"Town," I said. "Huddersfield Town."

"Will you remember that?" the gaffer asked. "Remember you're Huddersfield Town FC?"

"Yes, boss," I said.

"Do you think a fancy London team with a smart new stadium and rich men in its corridors deserves to beat us, Jack?"

"No," I said.

"That's right," he yelled. "Because when we are on the pitch, we're eleven men who can beat any team. Aren't we, Jack?"

"Yes, boss." I was smiling now. I felt different. Better.

The gaffer paused. Then he clenched his fists.

"I think Mr Norris has done my team talk for me," he said. "Is that right?"

Then the whole team was shouting, filling the corridors outside with our noise.

I knew then that we were going to hammer Arsenal.

FIVE

Huddersfield Town's first goal came from the wing.

Our winger moved away to the left and fired a low ball to me. But the Arsenal defence were tracking me close, so I drew them away from goal. Frank Mann found a pocket of space. He snapped up the pass and scored.

Bullock ran alongside me and slapped me on the back.

"Good work, Jack," he said.

Arsenal 0. Huddersfield Town 1.

The second goal came five minutes into the second half.

I started it. I thundered my way up field with the ball at my feet, then slipped a pass to another forward.

He shot.

The goalkeeper held it, but I hit him hard with my shoulder and he lost his balance. The ball spun across the goal mouth to Frank Mann, who tapped it home.

Arsenal 0. Huddersfield Town 2.

With minutes left, I decided to make my mark. I was happy to set up goals, but I wanted to score one too. I took a pass 40 yards out. But this time I didn't back into the defender and play it wide to the winger. I turned to take the Arsenal defence by surprise.

First I slipped past their captain, Chris Buckley. He tried to knock me off balance, but I shouldered him out of the way. When a second defender came

at me, I sped up and hit the ball hard towards the bottom corner.

When the goal went in, I felt an explosion inside me. All the bad thoughts and feelings of the day were blown to pieces. I had scored a great goal. I had also made an important decision.

Someone was waiting for me after the game. Not Norris, but Chris Buckley, the Arsenal captain.

"Well done, Jack," he said. His handshake was firm.

"Thank you."

"You had a good game," he said. "We couldn't cope with you." He let go of my hand, then slapped me on the shoulder. "See you again, son."

Bullock came up behind me as Chris Buckley left. "What did he say?" he asked.

I told him.

Bullock nodded. "That's a fine compliment."

"Thanks," I said. Then I hesitated. "Fred – about Norris?"

"What about him?" Bullock asked.

"He was right."

Fred's mouth fell open. "What? When he said that Huddersfield are a small-town team?"

"No," I said. "When he said I should sign up for the war, like you. I've made up my mind."

SIX

Two months after the Arsenal game, I arrived back in London. The football season was over.

I walked from Kings Cross station to the army office. If I was going to give up my freedom in exchange for service to the King, I wanted to take in London first. I threw my shoulders back and walked.

I had walked miles round London with Dad when I was a boy and we moved there from Cornwall, where I was born. He took me to museums, football matches and to watch the ships on the Thames. We always went by foot, happy to have the time to spend together. Especially on spring days like this one.

There was no doubt in my mind that I was doing the right thing. I had made a deal with myself – play the season out, then enlist. I was glad not to have to think about it any more, that I didn't still have a decision to make.

There was no queue at the Kingsway army offices. I thought I was the only man there until I heard someone call my name.

"Jack?"

I looked round to see two lads approaching. One was young and tall, with curly hair. The other was older, heavier. Percy Summers and Sid Wheelhouse. It was Summers' voice that I'd heard.

Wheelhouse was in his uniform. He'd been in the battalion for two months already. His body looked huge and powerful in his tunic. He grabbed my hand with a strong grip.

"Bullock said you'd be down here this week," he said. "Good to see you."

"And you," I said. "But what's this, Percy? Are you joining up today?"

Percy nodded. But there was something in his eyes – doubt or fear. I couldn't be sure. And he looked so young next to Wheelhouse.

"Right," Wheelhouse said. "I need to get over to the barracks at White City." He shook my hand again. "You two can sort each other out now."

Wheelhouse walked off, then turned to call back to us.

"Make sure you join the Footballers' Battalion and not any other. We need men like you to prove that footballers can fight. Yes?"

Percy and I nodded. Some newspaper men were still writing that footballers were cowards, that they couldn't fight. We had to prove them wrong.

When Wheelhouse had gone, Percy stood tall and breathed in deeply. I could tell he was nervous, so I waited for him to gather his thoughts.

"Come on," he said at last. "Let's go and sign this piece of paper."

A young officer wrote my details down as we sat in a great empty hall. There were rows of tables covered in paperwork, tables where men signed away their freedom. I ran my eyes down the form in front of me. It said, "SHORT SERVICE: for the duration of the war."

"Name?" the officer asked.

"Jack Cock."

"Address?" Then the officer put his pen down. "Just a moment," he said. "Are you a footballer?"

"Yes," I said. "I mean – yes, sir." At the last moment I'd remembered that this man was an

officer, my superior in the army world I was now part of.

He smiled. "I saw you," he said. "At Arsenal. That late goal you scored."

"Are you an Arsenal fan, sir?" Now it felt strange to be calling him "sir".

"I am." He frowned. "You finished our chances of promotion that day. Maybe we'll sign you after the war?"

"Maybe," I said as an older officer walked past our desk. Perhaps he had sensed the friendliness of our chat. The young officer picked up his pen.

"Address?" he asked again, a faint smile on his face.

"81 Ansell Street, Fulham."

"Are you a British subject?"

"Yes."

"Born in England?"

"Yes."

"You could be playing for England if it wasn't for this war," he said. "For some reason I thought you were a Scot, playing so far up north."

"No, sir. I'm English."

"Trade or calling?"

"Professional footballer."

"That you are," he said.

And then it struck me that when I signed this form I would no longer be a professional footballer. The thought made me sad. It was possible that I wouldn't kick a football again for months – for years. Maybe never.

The officer turned the form to face me, and placed his finger on the words – "Are you willing to serve upon the following conditions provided by His Majesty?"

He handed me his pen.

My heart beat hard, but I signed straight away.

Outside, I stood on the stone steps of the office to wait for Percy Summers. I slipped my hand into my pocket and pulled out my wallet. Inside I found the cartoon that Larrett Roebuck's widow had given me.

There's only one field where you can get honour.

Now I was going to discover if the cartoon was right.

PART 2
Volunteer

SEVEN

During my first days as a soldier, we marched. That was all. We marched up and down Bayswater Road. We marched with large packs. We marched with our new uniforms stiff around our backs, rubbing our necks raw.

Marching with packs was what war was about. We needed to be fit. We needed to carry things to war. We needed to do what we were told. Two weeks in, on a hot, humid day, I understood the real reason why they were training us to march.

That morning, we left White City barracks and headed for Marble Arch. Soldiers were grumbling. They were sick of marching back and forth in the sun.

Hyde Park was on our left as we marched back to the barracks. The happy summer smell of cut grass drifted through the city. And, on the other side of the railings, I saw two young women pushing prams, children playing ahead of them. Then three girls under parasols standing still, watching us. A couple of soldiers called out to them, but the corporals ordered them to keep quiet.

I didn't call out. I had just understood what we were doing. Those young women. Those children. They were the reason we were marching. So people like them would be free to walk in the parks. Free to be British.

That was why I had signed up to fight. Now I just had to get on with it.

After a month at White City barracks, the Footballers' Battalion moved on. To Surrey and

the grounds of a massive country house called Holmbury Park. We learned how to shoot, how to use a bayonet and how to throw bombs.

We spent the rest of the time digging.

Holmbury Park was quite a place – a huge building with windows that glowed golden in the summer sun. When we arrived there, I was made a corporal. That meant I had five men under me. It was my job to make sure they did what they were told. Which was, for the most part, digging.

We were scooping out a trench the day I met Frank Buckley, brother of the Arsenal captain, Chris. Frank was to change my life.

I was standing over the trench as Summers, Wheelhouse and three others followed the orders we'd been given earlier in the day to dig. The air was filled with the smell of the rich earth they had dug up. Percy Summers' face was black with soil and

his hair was dark with sweat. All the digging had made him muscly and strong. He looked nothing like the boyish goalkeeper I'd played against six months before.

"Can you see over the top?" I asked him.

He went up on the fire step and nodded.

"Good work," I said.

Then I saw Summers salute. At first I thought he was saluting me, until I saw some of the other men stand up with straight backs. And I knew there must be an officer behind me.

I turned to see Major Buckley, our battalion leader.

"At ease, men," he said. He kicked a stone across the top of the trench. "I need to speak to some of you. Something important has come up. Something very important."

"Yes, sir," I said.

We all stood to face him, ready for our orders.

"You will all have heard the rumours about a battalion football team. About a series of games. Yes?"

Nobody said anything.

"I see," Buckley said. "Well, the battalion is to hold trials tomorrow morning. Four games of one hour each. There will be no other duties or training until we have selected eleven men to play in the first of those games. Understood?"

"Yes, sir," I said, grinning.

Major Buckley grinned back at me.

EIGHT

Three hundred men were standing 200 yards from Holmbury Park's grand front entrance. But they weren't there to see the house or its gardens – they were there for the football. The outlines of a football pitch had been marked on the ground and now there were to be four short games, one after the other. Trials to choose men to represent the Footballers' Battalion in a series of matches across the country.

It was a chance to play football. To do something other than marching and digging. A chance to be footballers again – or to see them.

There was one player that the large crowd was desperate to see. Jack Woodward, the Chelsea striker. I was as keen as the rest of them – the man

was my hero. I'd seen him play a dozen times when I watched Chelsea before I moved to Huddersfield. He'd won a lot of honours and had played for England many times.

But now I would play against him. Jack Woodward was my rival for a place in the battalion team.

When I hit the pitch, I gave it everything. I felt fitter than ever. The army had done me some good, it seemed. It had made me stronger. And my touch was still there, fresher now I'd had a break from the game.

It all came flooding back. I liked being an army corporal, but I liked playing football more. This might be my last chance to be a footballer, and I wanted it. Even if it meant making my hero into my rival.

So I surged and powered through the other players, dropping back to collect the ball.

Bullock and Wheelhouse fed me pass after pass through the centre.

Sixty minutes later, I had scored three goals. I had made the impact I wanted to make. And I had – for an hour – forgotten about marching and digging.

After the four trials, the players from all the games – nearly one hundred of us – watched as Major Buckley came among us. We were all hoping for a tap on the shoulder.

"He's got to pick you," Summers said. "Here he comes."

I turned round to see Major Buckley behind me.

"The battalion has a match in Cardiff in a couple of weeks," he said. "I'd like to ask you to play centre forward."

"Yes, sir," I said. "I will, sir."

I was delighted. I was going to represent the British Army. In wartime, this was perhaps as close as I would ever get to my dream of playing for my country.

NINE

It was October when we went to Cardiff to play football in the Welsh mud at Ninian Park. The ground was between the city centre and the docks. The wind howled and clouds rushed across the sun.

I knew most of my battalion team-mates by now. We worked well together, even though we'd had no time to train.

But the match was frustrating. I had a Cardiff City defender on top of me all the time. He didn't give me a yard's space and I couldn't get forward. I wasn't dangerous enough. And I knew I needed to play harder, because there was more to this game than just playing for my battalion. It was a chance. There was a whisper that there were plans

for a great football tournament out in France, with teams drawn from each battalion, to keep the soldiers entertained when they were away from the trenches. It would be called the Flanders Cup. Matches would be played behind the trench lines.

It sounded unreal. But, if it was true, I wanted to be part of it. To play football was my dream – even in France, even at war. I knew I needed to work harder today to get into the game. Everyone was watching us. They would be making up their minds whether we could still play after weeks of digging and marching.

Even before the half-time whistle in Ninian Park, things were happening on the touchline. This was not just a game of football. A band was forming, with trumpets and tubas glinting in the sun. Buckley was there too, staring hard at the crowd, at the clusters of young men who had come to watch.

I knew Buckley cared about the game, about how well his team was doing, but his mind was elsewhere now. It was on the young men in the stands. He wanted to get them down from the stands. He wanted them to enlist to fight in France. That was what this football match was all about.

The moment the whistle blew for half-time, the band started to play. The music was fast and loud and rousing. Buckley was at the front, leading the singing. Hundreds joined in and drowned out the sound of any cheers as the players left the field.

We could hear the speeches from the dressing room under the stand.

"Men of Wales, join your brothers at the front! The war is nearly a year old. It did not end last Christmas. It will not end this Christmas. But, if you join up today, it could end next Christmas. Your country needs you."

I joined the rest of the players under the main stand to wait for the second half to begin. But an army captain was there at the head of the tunnel to hold us back. The speeches were still going on.

"Have you heard of the Battle of Loos? It was a setback for Britain and her allies. We can't afford any more setbacks like that one. We need men to sign up now. Like every one of the footballers in this brave Footballers' Battalion today. All heading for the front within days."

Joe Bailey.

Alan Foster.

And then I heard my own name read out as the name of a hero.

Be like Jack. Join up.

At the same time, I heard footsteps. Men were coming out of the crowd. They were roused by the music, roused by the speech of Major Frank Buckley.

Buckley had said we'd be heading for the front within days. But there was no time to think about that. At last, the army captain was letting us out of the tunnel and back onto the field of play. As men were herded into a large, empty stand to give their names, to hand themselves over to their country, I focused on playing football. I had to give it everything I had.

TEN

On the train back from Cardiff, Buckley came to find me. I was sitting with some of the other men and one of them was telling me I was a clear choice for the next battalion game, even though I hadn't scored that day. Then Buckley was there.

"Corporal," Buckley said as he slid the door of our compartment open. "A word."

Outside in the corridor, he smiled at me.

"I've been watching you, son," he said. "At the barracks. At Holmbury Park. And I like you. You hold the ball up well. You've got power in the air. You're hard to knock off the ball. And you've got an eye for goal."

I could have listened to him talking like that all day. But there was something in his voice that told me there was a "but" coming. Or a "however".

"There are two battalion games left," he said, "before we go."

Now I was listening. Before we go where – to France?

"But I've decided to play Captain Woodward in those games," Buckley went on. "He's a better name than you this side of the war, son. He can draw a bigger crowd. He can help us recruit."

My head dropped. Jack Woodward had won in the end and now I had no idea when I would play another game of football. If I ever did.

I felt desperate, but I saluted the Major.

"Sir?" I said. "You said 'before we go'. Do you know when that will be?"

"November the 16th, Corporal. Two weeks' time. Can you tell the other men? They'll be keen to know."

"Yes, sir," I said.

Once Buckley had gone, I returned to my team-mates. I had a lot to tell them.

Two weeks later, I stood in front of Buckley again. This time, I was standing with the 300 men of the Footballers' Battalion, B Company. Wheelhouse, Summers and Bullock were beside me. We were on Platform 1 of Salisbury railway station, waiting beside a train that would take us to the south coast of England. From there, we would sail to France.

"Gentlemen. We are about to embark on a journey to war. I'm not going to pretend it's going to be easy. It will not be easy. Nor, for that matter, will it be pleasant."

As Buckley spoke, there was a dead silence across the station, except for a burst of steam now and then from one of the engines and the sound of birds singing on the roof.

"This war we are going to fight will become known as the greatest war in history," Buckley told us. "In years to come, when people think of soldiers, they will think of you. They will see you in your uniforms, with your packs on your backs and your rifles in your hands, and they will remember what you did.

"You have just marched through the finest country in the world to this station. Through the fields and lanes of Britain. One day, we will come home from this war. One day, we will walk again down English lanes. One day, we will tell our children and our grandchildren about what we have done. And they will come to know that we did it for

them. That we did it for the families and the values of Britain.

"Of course, some of you men here will not return to walk down an English lane."

I saw Buckley pause after saying this. We knew what was coming next. A punch line. Something to make us think.

"Those men, the ones who do not return, they will be the real heroes."

Buckley paused again.

"Some people," he said, "have said in speeches and written in the newspapers that footballers cannot be heroes, that footballers don't have what it takes in the field of war."

Another pause. I swear I could hear 300 men holding their breath.

"We'll see about that," Buckley shouted. Then he stepped back down onto the platform.

The noise that greeted the end of his speech was astonishing. It began as a cheer and ended as a war cry. It shocked me. And what shocked me most was that I was part of it.

ELEVEN

The train journey from Salisbury to Folkestone
took for ever. The men were restless and bored.
I sat with my friends from the football field, men
who would soon stand beside me on the field of
war. I was happy to have Bullock with me. He was a
corporal, like me. But to me he would always be my
captain and my leader.

It was a blowy November night. Rain spattered
on the windows of the carriage. Earlier, there had
been a view of fields and lanes, but now there was
only blackness.

But as I peered into the blackness, I realised
I was wrong to think there was nothing to see.
The dark window showed me a carriage full of

men, dressed in khaki uniforms, with packs on the racks above them. Some were chatting. Some were laughing. Clouds of smoke rose around them as they lit cigarette after cigarette to cope with the boredom – or with their nerves.

Wheelhouse, Bullock and Summers were staring out into the darkness like me.

I stood up to open the carriage window, enjoying the cold fresh air as it flooded in.

"Have you been on a ship before?" I asked my three mates, wanting to break the silence. All three shook their heads.

Then we heard a laugh from behind us and a soldier's face appeared over the back of our seats. It was Jackie Sheldon. We knew him. He'd been up on a charge of match fixing when he was at Liverpool.

"It's not the ships you have to worry about," he said. "Nor the sea."

"What, then?" Summers asked. Now he was cleaned up and wedged between Wheelhouse and Bullock, he looked like a boy again.

"Submarines," Sheldon whispered. "German U-boats, searching for ships to sink. Ships like ours."

"So I hear," Wheelhouse spat back. "But best not think about that, eh?" There was a dark malice in his voice. Wheelhouse stole a look at Summers – he knew that the younger man was worried about the subs.

But Sheldon was still talking. "Hospital ship went down last night," he said. "Summers, did you hear that? They got a hospital ship with a torpedo last night. Three hundred dead. But not dead like alive, then dead. Dead after hours in the water. Frozen to death. Imagine that. In the sea, the cold gripping your legs, then your arms, then your chest, then ..."

Wheelhouse was on his feet now. "Get out, Sheldon," he barked.

One look at Wheelhouse, and Sheldon ran. Fast.

After that there was no more talk, no more laughing. The whole carriage was quiet. I looked out of the window at the blackness, trying to make out features of the landscape. But it was so dark that the train felt like it was at the bottom of the sea.

PART 3
Soldier

TWELVE

We walked down the gangplank and set foot for the first time in France.

Most of us had never walked on foreign soil before. We'd only been on the ship for 90 minutes – the length of a football match – and now we were in another country.

As I walked across the cobbles of the French port, all I felt was relief. Relief that we were in control of our lives again. Out there on the boat, in the dark, a torpedo could have blown us up or pitched us into the sea at any moment. We would have been helpless, with no chance of survival.

But the relief vanished when we saw the men who were waiting to return to Britain. The lucky

ones had bandages around their heads or their legs or their arms. Some were slumped in wheelchairs. Others were shells of men, lying broken on stretchers.

That night we marched through Boulogne, a French town the Germans had not yet taken. I marched ahead of the five men I was responsible for as corporal – Summers, Wheelhouse, Page, Mawson and Evans.

We marched for several hours and then we boarded a train. It was a filthy old thing that normally would have been used to move animals around. There were perhaps a thousand men to load onto the one train – sixty men per cattle truck. When it was our turn to board, I made sure all my men were in the truck before me.

"I don't think much of these first-class carriages, sir," Evans joked.

"Don't open the door unless we stop at a station," a Sergeant Major ordered. "Only on a platform. Understood?"

"Yes, sir," I said.

Some of the men sat down. Others stood and tried to peer out of the small holes in the sides of the trucks.

All the jokes stopped once the doors were locked shut. The only sound was the clanging of chains between the trucks. The smell was horrendous.

We could tell that the train was stopping when we felt our truck nudge into the one in front. I peered out of the gap in the door, searching for a sign to tell us where we were.

Saint-Omer.

The light was bright when we opened the doors. When our eyes adjusted, we saw a crowd standing on the platform. There were women, children and

old men. They were holding jugs of steaming hot chocolate and some kind of bread. For us.

I passed the food and drink to the soldiers behind me, then took my turn.

"Merci," I said.

The girl serving me grinned and blushed. The hot chocolate filled my body with warmth. But the bread was the best bit. Sweet, warm and flaky – it melted in my mouth. I had never eaten anything like it.

"Croissant," the girl said. She pointed to the bread, offering more.

"Croissant," I repeated.

The girl threw her arms around me for a moment, then drew away. During that two-second embrace I understood what we meant to these people. We were there to stop the Germans taking their land, their houses and their lives.

Our next stop would be the trenches.

THIRTEEN

We were on another night march. In the rain, soaked to the skin. The wool of our uniforms was heavy and sodden. Our boots leaked. Our feet were soaked.

I could see our column of men ahead of me, marching up the hill and dipping into the next shallow valley. Behind, I could see the same. Hundreds of men. Thousands of men. Marching to war.

Onward Christian soldiers, marching as to war ...

Where had I heard those words? Back in Huddersfield? Or Cardiff? I couldn't remember. All

that had happened in Britain seemed so long ago, so far away.

Then Summers was beside me.

"There's a storm coming," he said.

"What's that?"

"I heard thunder. And I saw lightning," he told me. "There must be a storm coming this way. But I don't suppose we can get any wetter than we already are."

I looked east. For a moment there was nothing. The men were moving quietly, like they were marching in their sleep. I wished it was morning. We would feel better when it was light.

And then I saw a flash and heard a long, rumbling echo.

But it wasn't thunder. Or lightning. It was the blast of a shell – the never-ending shellfire that the two armies in the trenches hurled at each other. I

wondered what to say to Summers. Should I pretend that all we were seeing was an electrical storm? No, I couldn't lie to him.

"Percy," I said.

"Yes?"

"That's not a storm. It's –"

Summers interrupted. "I know, Jack. I know what it is."

As he looked at the flickering lights cast by the exploding shells, I had to shake my head to remind myself this wasn't a bad dream. We really were marching towards them.

We spent the next day sitting in a field beside a place that must once have been a large farmyard. At the highest point of the field there was a deep trench. I had been watching men coming and going from the tunnel all day. Carrying ammunition, food,

jars, bottles, shells, stretchers with men lying on them. Everything and everyone coming out was covered in mud.

And now it was our turn to go in.

We walked in single file. It was the only way to walk into the trench system. The walls were narrow. It was so dark all we could do was follow the next man.

As we walked, we watched where we put our feet. If we fell, our kit and rifles would get filthy and it would take hours to clean them.

The change was startling when a flare went up. For a few seconds we could see clearly. There were still black shadows deeper down and – under the wooden duck-boards – something moving.

Was it a play of the light?

No. We knew exactly what it was.

Rats.

FOURTEEN

The front line was a place where I'd expected to be overcome by fear. It was less than 300 yards from the Germans and their guns. But I had five men to think about. Those men took my mind off my fears for myself.

I gathered them into a huddle, so close that our faces were almost touching.

"Right," I said, in a low voice. "Mawson, Page, Summers – try and sleep. Wheelhouse and Evans, you stay awake. Have your bayonets fixed in case we're attacked. I'll do the first hour look-out."

When you were on look-out, you had to stare out across No Man's Land, with your head and shoulders above the parapet. You were watching

for movement, listening for sounds of Germans creeping towards you with bombs, tunnelling under the trenches. Small groups of Germans even roamed No Man's Land in the hope of taking one of us hostage.

My five men looked at me.

"But you're the corporal," Mawson whispered.

"So?" I asked.

"So you can make one of us be the look-out."

"And I will," I said. "But if I have to ask you to do it, I'm going to do it first."

And then I put my fingers on my lips to silence them. I knew nothing about standing in the line of fire or leading men. I had no experience. So I chose to do what I thought my dad would have done. He would have gone first and so I did the same.

I put on my tin helmet and placed my foot up onto the fire step to move into position.

The first thing I felt up there was the wind moving across the surface of No Man's Land, carrying the stench of mud and burning. Ahead was blackness. There could easily have been a kidnap party of Germans lying there on their bellies, a sniper aiming his rifle at my head, or a shell about to explode in my face. I could see nothing.

I felt exposed. But it wasn't the dark that made me feel that way – it was the silence. The silence was so extraordinary that even a click in our own trench a hundred yards away made my heart race.

But I had no choice. I had to deal with feeling exposed, with the terror of the silent darkness around me.

Once my eyes became accustomed to the night, it didn't seem so dark. Now I began to see things. The outlines of splintered trees. Rolls of barbed wire, attached to stakes driven into the ground.

The cratered ground ahead of me. Some of the dangers I had feared were not there. Others, I could do nothing about. So I thought about my parents, composing a letter to them in my head.

Dear Mum and Dad. We have reached the front line at last. The lads are glad to be here. We'd been marching for days and everyone is eager to have a go at the Germans ...

Suddenly I saw something to my left. I turned my head slowly, trying to avoid any sudden movement that would make me visible from the German trenches. I saw another soldier turning his head to stare back at me, along our line.

Private John MacDonald. One of Bullock's men.

I could only just make out his face, but I thought I saw him wink. So I winked back and felt a little less alone. If I just stood like this, not moving, not

speaking, it would eventually be dawn and time for the next round of orders. That was all I had to do.

Time passed. I saw nothing move. I heard nothing other than the whispers of men and the wind singing in the barbed wire.

Then a crack, louder than the cracks that had come before.

A thud.

A shout. "He's been hit ..."

The shout had come from the next section. Bullock's section.

I looked across, but there was no sign of MacDonald. I thought he must have ducked down. So I ducked down too, into the bottom of the trench, just as Evans came at me round the corner.

"They've hit Mac," he shouted.

I looked around me. My five men were all frozen in fear. What should they do now? They were

looking at me for an answer. I dashed out of my section and into Bullock's. I almost ran into Bullock, who was holding up a lantern.

"What is it?" I shouted. "What's happened?"

"MacDonald's dead," he said, his eyes filled with rage. "Shot through the head."

As he moved aside, I saw three of his men on the bottom of the trench, looking down at MacDonald. John MacDonald, the man who'd winked at me not an hour before. He had a hole in his head, above his eye. A mess of blood was pumping out of the back of his head, pooling in the mud. His face was pale. There was dark blood coming out of his gaping mouth.

I felt my legs go beneath me, but I managed to steady myself on the trench wall. It was a horrible thing to see a man dead, just like that. I found it hard to believe it had really happened.

I put my hand on Bullock's shoulder for a second, then turned to walk back to my unit. All eyes were on me. Well, almost all. Summers was looking around in a panic, searching for a way out.

"MacDonald is dead," I said, desperate not to show my men my shock and horror. I swallowed. "A sniper hit him. He died instantly."

No one had anything to say. The silence was painful. Once again, the only sound was the wind in the barbed wire.

And that sound drew my mind to No Man's Land. I remembered that someone was supposed to be watching it, keeping a look-out for kidnap parties, lone bombers, gas attacks. So I spoke into Mawson's ear, told him to keep an eye on Summers. Then I put my foot on the fire step to ease myself up. And there was No Man's Land again. Unchanged.

I kept myself as still as I possibly could, in that vast desert of craters, tree stumps, mud and death.

FIFTEEN

A typical day began with colours rippling the darkness on the horizon. It was calm. It was quiet. Then, just as the sky changed, we heard the first cracks of sniper fire.

We faced east, so sunrise was the only time of day that we had the advantage over the Germans.

As the faintest glimmer of light crept across the sky, we could sometimes see a German head above the parapet. That was when we had our rifles ready. We slipped the gun through a loophole in the trench side. There was a cloth behind us, so we could not be seen.

And that was when we fired. The *snap snap* of bullets across No Man's Land.

We never knew if we had hit a German.

Had they dodged our bullet? Or had it hit them, metal ripping into flesh? Were they now lying on the floor of their trench, their body in a death spasm, like MacDonald? Did their comrades stand hopelessly around them like we had done?

We never knew. But we had to try to kill them. If we didn't kill them, then they would kill us.

But life in the trenches was not all about guns, bullets and bombs. It was about being cold and wet and filthy and itchy. Our bodies were covered in lice that we could never shake off, however hard we tried.

Some men found ways to stop the boredom driving them insane. They declared war on an enemy even closer to home than the Germans.

The rats.

I didn't take part in the ratting. I preferred to pretend they weren't there. But they were. They scuttled beneath our feet and skipped over us as we slept. They were always looking for food. They gnawed their way into our packs or into treats sent from home. They ate fruit cake, tobacco – everything. Once we even had to watch them eat a German soldier.

The German soldier had tried to sneak up to our trenches one night with a bag full of bombs. He wanted to kill us all.

But the rules of war state – kill the killer before he kills you. And so Wheelhouse shot him. But once he was dead, we felt nothing but pity for him. His corpse was ten yards from us, out there in No Man's Land. It didn't smell. It was winter. It was freezing, and frozen bodies don't rot.

So it wasn't the smell of the German that was the problem. It was the rats nesting in his ribcage. They ate away most of his stomach and his face. We could see them moving inside him. Eating. Breeding. Preening themselves. Then they would run back into the trenches from the holes they'd made in that poor German soldier.

So perhaps it was no wonder that some of our men were more interested in fighting the rats than the Germans.

Cheese was the favourite weapon in the rat war. Mawson was excellent at this hunting method. First he fixed his bayonet to his rifle. Then he skewered a piece of cheese on the end of the bayonet. Next he put the tip of the bayonet facing out into No Man's Land and held it there.

The rats weren't timid. It wouldn't be long before one would come creeping out of the mud and

filth and make its way up to the parapet. At first the rat would be careful, but soon its whiskers would tremble with excitement.

Then it would come closer. Sniff. Lick its lips. Nibble at the cheese.

That's when I would hear the crack of Mawson's rifle and smell the burning powder from his gun. I would look up to see the rat scattered in pieces of red and brown flesh and fur.

But, amid this horror, something good was coming. Something I never really believed would happen. Not here, out in France, in the trenches – and in the midst of war. That something was football. A football tournament.

SIXTEEN

The Flanders Cup. A football tournament between all the battalions.

The trenches were alive with rumours that the generals had said yes to the Cup. They wanted to give the men something else to think about other than shells exploding above them and snipers trying to shoot them.

Everyone in the British Army was excited about the idea. But the Flanders Cup meant even more to our battalion. This was our chance to prove that footballers could fight and keep playing too. We wanted to win at war and at football.

But there were other rumours in the trenches as well. One time we heard that the Germans had

abandoned their positions and were sending in shellfire from miles away. Another time we heard that they were burrowing their way to Paris with tunnelling machines. Until a rumour was proved true we didn't give it a minute of our time. That was the only way we could cope with life on the front line. Hope was too dangerous. And so was fear.

But then we heard that Major Frank Buckley was in the trenches and that he was moving down the line telling men face to face that they were in the team. That they were the men he had selected to represent the Footballers' Battalion in the Flanders Cup.

Jack Woodward had been picked. Joe Bailey and Fred Bullock were in too.

"Do you reckon we're in as well?" Summers asked me.

"I don't know," I said.

"There's no way they'd leave you out," Summers said.

I shrugged, then went back to cleaning my rifle. It needed to be perfect. My next shot might be the most important one of my life.

The next time I looked up, I saw that Major Buckley was standing over me. He didn't need to speak to tell me that I was in.

SEVENTEEN

In the first game of the Flanders Cup, we beat the Essex Battalion and I scored two goals.

That game was a relief – because we had won well, because we had proved that those people who said footballers couldn't fight in the trenches and play football were wrong.

But it was more than a relief. It was a joy. A complete and utter thrill to play football again. I was determined to play that match like it was my last ever game.

Buckley, Bullock, Wheelhouse and Woodward were all in the team. There were others I didn't know, like the Reading forward, Joe Bailey.

The game came down the wings, because the mud was deeper in the middle of the pitch. That way we could avoid the worst of it. That suited Bailey very well. The ball came to me either as high balls from Wheelhouse and Bullock, or from the right off Bailey on the wing.

The Essex boys played a simple system. They sat deep and let us have the space, then came at us as soon as we were in their penalty area.

But I was strong after weeks of wading through the muddy water of the trenches. I was one of the biggest men on the pitch. I moved through the mud faster than any of the others.

The final score was 9–0.

After the game, Buckley brought us together in a huddle. We were covered in mud, and cold rain was sweeping across the French fields, but we didn't care.

"Well played, men," Buckley said. "That was a good show, but the Staffs are up next. And they'll be tougher opponents. We may not win nine–nil again."

To be honest, I didn't care about the score. I was part of a team that was pulling together to win a game of football. That was enough for me.

Only Jack Woodward wasn't really part of the team. We all knew he would want to have a talk with Buckley after the game. We didn't realise just how dramatic that talk would be.

After Buckley's huddle, my limbs were heavy and steam was coming off me like a horse after a run. I needed to try and dry off, but Buckley signalled me to wait behind. He was excited. I could see it in his eyes.

He said I was a revelation. He said that his brother, the Arsenal captain, had spoken of me. And now Buckley himself had seen me in action.

Then he was making promises. When this war was all over, he would be a football manager. He would build a team around me – a team that would win the league. He would make sure I played in the top flight, and more than that, he would make sure I was the top scorer too. He'd make sure I played for England.

It was exactly what I wanted to hear. It gave me that feeling I used to have – that my future was in football. That I could play at the top level. But then I saw that someone else had been listening to Buckley's words of praise. Someone out of Buckley's field of vision, but not mine.

It was Jack Woodward. He was wearing the same football colours – and the same shade of mud – as

the rest of us, but he looked different. His face and hair were as clean as they had been at the start of the game. He looked like a gentleman.

"Major Buckley," Woodward shouted.

"Woodward," Buckley said, turning to see him there. "Well played ..."

Woodward flushed with anger. "Don't say 'well played' to me," he snapped. "I didn't play damn well. I didn't get a chance. The whole team was playing to this man, not me. All the supply was going his way. I was on his shoulder for 90 minutes and he didn't play me in once."

He was right. I hadn't played him in. I had wanted the ball all for myself. I was the stronger player now. Woodward was not the player he used to be.

Buckley took a second to answer. "It was the mud," he said at last. I knew what Buckley was

doing – he wanted to calm Woodward down and draw attention away from me.

"It was the mud," he said again. "There was nothing coming down the middle for you, Woodward. The mud meant you barely had a touch."

EIGHTEEN

After that game, Jack Woodward was a different man. He had – I heard – registered for a new job. That job was bomb clearance and it wasn't something anyone normally volunteered for.

Our trenches were so close to the German trenches that it wasn't that difficult for one side to creep out over the parapet on dark nights. With a bag full of hand bombs to toss into the other side's trenches. Men had been killed by live grenades falling and exploding on them. It was a constant threat. But sometimes they didn't explode and someone had to clear them away.

That was Woodward's new job. He had gone from hero on the pitch to hero in the trenches. He

had stepped forward and put his life in danger to save the lives of others.

I was in the trench one night, trying to sleep in the endless rain, when I heard a wet thud.

We all looked down at our feet.

And there it was. A stick grenade.

Summers dived away from it. Wheelhouse and I stood stock still, just staring. Mawson and Evans dodged out of the trench.

The grenade didn't explode.

Woodward came to clear it, hurling it into No Man's Land, where it failed to explode for a second time.

"Thank you, sir," I said, when he allowed us back into our section.

"You're welcome, Corporal."

The next time I saw Woodward was when a bomb bounced into Bailey's section of trench. When

it didn't go off – another dud – Woodward and his team came to clear it. Woodward ordered his men to retreat and went about his work. The next thing we knew there was an explosion and a shower of soil poured down on us.

I dashed into the section of trench Woodward had been clearing, just as Bullock did the same from the other side. And there was Woodward, his back arched, his face twisted in agony from a long deep wound I could see through his shredded trousers. Blood covered his uniform and was splashed across his face.

Bullock held Woodward's head still as I tied a strap round his leg to stop the bleeding, trying to keep it tight as my fingers ran wet with his sticky blood. Someone else, maybe Summers, shouted for the stretcher-bearer. Once I'd tied the strap,

I looked away from Woodward's leg, checking the trench around me, making sure it was secure.

Woodward seemed calm. His eyes were on mine all that time. So I kept my eyes on his. I kept him talking too. I wanted to make sure he stayed awake.

"The bearers will be here soon," I said. "It's been a quiet night. You'll be fine."

"Look at my leg, Corporal," Woodward ordered.

I hadn't looked at it since tying the strap. I hadn't looked because I knew that if I looked he would ask me about it. And that was something I wanted to avoid.

"Look," he said again.

I looked.

"What are my injuries, Corporal?"

"You've two injures, sir. Both above the knee. The bleeding has slowed now."

"And how bad are the injuries, Corporal?"

I had a second to decide what to tell him. I could say they were minor injuries and that he might play football again. Or I could tell him the truth – his wounds were serious. He would live, but his legs were ruined. His footballing career was over. I looked in his eyes and I knew I had to tell him the truth.

"The injuries are deep, sir. Not life-threatening. But your legs are badly damaged."

Woodward smiled at me through his pain. "Thank you, Corporal," he said.

I was impressed by that smile. Woodward was in terrible pain. I had just told him that his career was over. But he had been polite to me. He was a brave and honourable man.

NINETEEN

There was tension in the trenches – a sense of anticipation. It was the 11th of June 1916.

Men were being asked to go out into No Man's Land. Joe Bailey, Percy Summers, Major Buckley and I were among them.

The night before, three men had been out to lay mines under a shallow dip in the ground within hearing distance of the Germans. The whole trench held their breath as the mining party did their work.

They were lucky. There were no stars that night and the wind was howling. They were neither seen nor heard.

It was a successful mission.

But tonight was different. The plan was simple. Two mines would blow two great craters in the mud. We would move out into No Man's Land and use the craters as cover, then throw grenades into the German trenches. It was the battalion's most important attack so far and we wanted to get it right.

I looked out across No Man's Land with a periscope – two mirrors on a stick that allowed me to see without having my head shot off. No Man's Land was a strange terrain. This area had once been a brickworks. Some stacks of bricks still stood around. A few stray bricks were scattered across the ground. And the mud was red, coloured by smashed brick dust.

"Right, men," a young lieutenant called Bradstreet said. "A period of shelling will stop at 22:53 hours on the dot. Then the two mines will blow.

The minute we hear them go off, I will count to five. On five, I'll blow my whistle and ... and we go over. We take the craters."

Lieutenant Bradstreet was good at breaking things down into steps. First we will do one thing, then a second thing and a third thing, then a fourth thing will happen. But we all knew it wouldn't be like that. Fifth and sixth and seventh things would happen too. And none of us could predict what those things would be.

The moon was out that night. There was no cloud cover. The Germans would be able to see us as soon as the showers of earth and brick dust stopped. And nobody really believed that they would let us waltz over to within 30 yards of their trenches.

"They'll come at us," I said to Bailey. "They'll want to take those craters as much as we do."

"They will," he agreed. "But we'll be in there first. We'll be ready. We'll be faster. We want them more."

TWENTY

At 22:45 hours on the night of the crater attack, every man was given a tot of rum and ordered to fix their bayonet blades onto their guns.

I fixed mine as fast as I could, then watched the five men in my section following my example. Then I looked back at the end of my own bayonet again.

How many times had I stuck it into a straw man? Stomach first, then a twist before I pulled it out. I always knew there would come a day I might have to use it on a real person. Perhaps it would be today.

I wasn't afraid. I knew that when I was faced with a German, I would kill him. I also knew he'd be perfectly capable of doing the same to me.

Everyone in my section of the trench was quiet now.

The scream of shells coming from behind our lines and the blasts ahead of us had been going on for so many hours that they had become background noise. So when the guns did stop, the silence made a painful ringing and hissing noise in my ears.

Then it came – BOOM-BOOM. A double explosion. The whole earth shook. Soil and bricks showered down on us as we squatted to avoid the worst of it, knowing we only had seconds left.

Then we heard Lieutenant Bradstreet's voice above the noise.

"Two … three … four … five."

His whistle.

Nothing like a referee's whistle, I thought.

Football. It wasn't a time to be thinking about football.

And then Bradstreet scrambled up a ladder, stuck his head above the parapet and scrambled into No Man's Land. The rest of us were right behind him, our bayonets out in front of us, blinded by the flares the Germans had sent up.

I kept low as I ran. My helmet was over my eyes. The ground was so uneven and sodden that I had to adjust my balance with every footfall. It was more like wading than running, with all that mud. What I remember most is two sounds. The first was my breathing, so loud it seemed it was coming from someone running beside me. And the second was the screech of bullets whipping through the air around me, like invisible flies. If they hit me, they would knock me over, rip into my skin and flesh and muscle, shatter my bones.

When my foot landed on something more uneven than soil or brick or mud, I looked down to see a uniform, an arm, a face screwed up in pain.

Summers.

It was Percy Summers. Dying in the mud.

I didn't stop. I wasn't allowed to stop. My orders were to keep going.

Rule 1. Never stop to help a fellow soldier when you're attacking, even though every sinew in your body wants to help him.

The air was full of bullets as I ran. It sounded like someone was lashing the air with dozens of whips. Machine guns rattled on my left. There were lights everywhere. I had no idea what they were. Or where they were. And then I was punched on the side of the head and I fell.

Who would punch me? Germans wouldn't punch me. They'd run me through with their bayonets, spilling my guts across the mud.

The man who was running behind me trod on my shoulder and pushed my face down into the mud. That brought me back to my senses. It didn't matter what had hit me. What mattered was that I had to go on.

I scrambled back to my feet. I was running again. I wasn't dead. Not yet.

I'd lost time falling over and being trodden on. The others were ahead of me, black shapes running, falling, disappearing into the crater.

And there it was. The crater, up ahead. I ran harder still. And then at last I was over the rim of the crater and down. Buckley was there – he handed grenades to me and Lieutenant Bradstreet without a word.

"Thirty yards," Bradstreet said, pointing. "Aim at the sparks."

I knew the target. It was a machine gun, coughing bullets, spitting fire.

I lobbed a first grenade. It fell short.

I lobbed a second. Closer.

I aimed again. But now there were soldiers in my line of fire. I was about to call to them to move out of the way when the light of a flare flashed off their blades.

Germans.

Germans with bayonets fixed, suddenly lit up by a pair of flares sent up to show them where we were hiding in the dark. But the flares meant we could see them too.

Buckley handed me more grenades. I had to keep on throwing, trusting that other men would kill the Germans. And, indeed, before the Germans

reached me, other black shapes reared up. I heard the clash of blades. I saw men fall, twisting backwards. I heard the machine gun again and I lobbed another bomb. The flames and the debris and the sparks stopped.

I'd hit it.

I'd taken out one of their guns.

But the machine-gun fire didn't stop. There was another gun to my left. More sparks and strange lights.

I moved along the length of the crater with Lieutenant Bradstreet. I pulled grenades from my pockets and gave them to him.

Bullets fizzed through the air, soil fell in our eyes and hair, shouts echoed around us, but we kept throwing until all the grenades had gone. All the Germans coming at us from above had been stabbed

and now there was only their bubbling, murmuring, screaming, crying left to disturb us.

One last machine gun hammered away in the night, followed by silence.

A lull.

No more hand-to-hand fighting.

No more bayoneting.

No more bombs.

Then I thought I could make out one voice among all the others, above the noise of shells and bullets whipping through the air. Summers. It was coming from the place I had seen him fall.

Buckley was lying next to me, his head low. Bradstreet too.

"I can hear Summers," I said, above the din as the machine gun started up again. "I know where he is. Permission to go back and bring him in, sir?"

Buckley shook his head.

"Please, sir," I insisted. "I know his position."

I looked hard at Buckley's muddied face until I saw in his eyes that he had changed his mind.

"Get back to the fire trench," he shouted. "It's his best chance."

TWENTY-ONE

Machine-gun bullets burned in the air above me as I crawled and slithered across the mud. Flares were going up. I could sense the Germans looking out from their trenches, rifles trained on anyone that moved among the dead and the dying, anything they could see in the carnage of No Man's Land.

I had to concentrate on Summers. I hoped to find him and save him. But he might not be alive. He'd been out there – shot – for some time.

What if he was dead?

I had an answer for that too. If he was dead, I wanted to get him back to our lines. I wanted his mum and dad to have his body to bury. We all knew that bodies left out in No Man's Land sank

into the mud when the rats had stripped them. If this war ever came to an end, if this deadly land could ever be farmed again, their only chance of a proper grave would be to be turned up by a farmer's plough.

I had to find him.

Thirty yards, I reckoned. I counted them out.

And there he was. I looked at the heavy wound in his chest, making sure I didn't let my face change, making sure I didn't let him understand that he might die.

Summers made a noise back, but the shape of the words got lost in his pain.

I turned him over, keeping low, out of reach of bullets. I put his gun and my gun on his back and tied them down. Then I began to move backwards, pulling him after me, inch by inch.

After half an hour I was shattered. It was the most exhausting thing I had ever done. If anyone had asked me to play football now, I wouldn't have been able to do it. But I put that thought away. For once, I didn't care about football. All I cared about was getting my friend back to our lines.

An hour later, No Man's Land fell silent. Our crater party had retreated back to our lines. Those of them who had survived. It was just me and Summers out there now.

The quiet made it deadly dangerous. There was no other noise to hide our movements. And every time I moved Summers, he groaned. I had patched him up, but he still had a filthy hole in his chest, probably a bullet lodged in there too.

We were over halfway back to the trenches when it all went wrong. I pulled Summers over a rock or a root. He cried out in agony.

Immediately a series of flares lit the sky over us.

I got down and lay still. Dead still, like a corpse. Summers and I were both coated in mud. Our uniforms, our bare skin – thick with mud and blood. We were as well hidden as we could be – just two more corpses out in that terrible place.

The Germans would see nothing. They wouldn't know where we were.

Then I heard the pop of mortars being fired. They were sending up mortar bombs to come down on No Man's Land. These bombs were random attempts to hit us, or to put us off coming out into the hellish muddy blackness again.

Summers and I got back to the trench three hours later than the rest of the battalion.

They had held the crater for two hours, then scrambled home. Summers was still alive when the stretcher-bearers arrived to take him to the field hospital.

All the men who'd made it back were slumped with their helmets and guns still on, too tired to do anything but sleep. After we had taken stock of our losses, after replacements had been called up from the reserve trenches, after we'd had our breakfast and our rum, Major Buckley came round to speak to the men.

"Seven dead or missing," he said. "Bradstreet, for one. But we hit them hard."

Buckley eyed me then. It was a fierce stare, but I had no idea what he was thinking, or what he was about to say. He knew I wanted to know about Summers. Had the stretcher-bearers saved him? Or had I been too late?

My heart beat faster as Buckley spoke.

"Summers is going to live," he said. "You did well, Corporal. You saved that man's life. I am going to recommend you for a decoration. The Military Medal."

"Will he go back to England, sir?" I asked, not really hearing what he had said about the medal. The idea of a medal seemed absurd.

"He will, Corporal."

I was glad. Summers would be safe in England.

"And, Corporal?" Buckley went on.

"Yes, sir?"

"There's a large dent in your helmet."

I reached up to touch my helmet, then I took it off. The Major was right. There was a dent made by a bullet that the helmet must have deflected away.

And then I understood. I hadn't been punched out there – I'd been shot.

TWENTY-TWO

Three days after the crater attack, they brought us back from the front line of trenches. We were shattered. Our bodies and minds had been stretched as far as they could go.

We should have wanted to rest, but what we wanted was to play football. We wanted to get away from the trenches and be footballers again. Maybe we thought that if we could be footballers, then we wouldn't have to be soldiers.

The crowd was larger for the next game, against the Staffordshire Regiment. There were 3,000 men crowded round a field marked out with white lines, surrounded by deep horse tracks and piles of empty supply boxes. They were there to forget the war

they'd just left, the war they'd soon head back to again.

Parts of the pitch were six inches deep in mud. The ball barely bounced – but I felt like I was flying. It helped that I had played with some of the other men before.

Joe Bailey was on the right wing. Sid Wheelhouse and Fred Bullock were at the back. Together they were like a locked barn door.

And Major Buckley was part of the team too. That was what we were – a team. A real team.

The game was over by half-time. 3–0.

I scored twice and Bailey once. Both of my goals came from solo runs. I drew the defenders, played the ball ahead of them so it stuck in the mud, and then I shouldered past them to clip the ball past the keeper. The defenders tried to tackle me – with their arms, not their feet.

The second half passed the same as the first. Three goals for. None against.

Near the end, Bailey took to the touchline and crossed the ball in to me. We knew that way I could score headers. There's nothing like the feeling of hitting a ball off your forehead, to see it rocket into the back of the goal.

The plan worked. I scored two more. Each time I headed the ball, the sodden, muddy weight of it nearly knocked me out. My face was spattered in so much filthy water, I could barely see. But each time I felt myself laughing for the joy of it. I felt like a boy again.

For 90 minutes I forgot the shellfire, the rats, the Germans, the rain, the cold and the fear I felt when I was above the parapet, listening to the night.

Staffordshire Regiment 0. Footballers' Battalion 6.

And now I wanted more.

TWENTY-THREE

Before we went back to the front line, they had a task for us – to take Delville Wood. Once we had control of it, we would be closer to the German trenches beyond.

We were told that the assault would make a huge difference to the war effort. We were told that hundreds of other units had gone in to weaken the German lines. We weren't told what had happened to them.

As we moved through the wood, shells flew overhead and we could hear bursts of machine-gun fire in the distance. Most of the trees had been burned black. A few were split open, baring their white flesh. Flesh that would soon be scorched.

There was no way through the trees and the undergrowth. Everything was covered in a mess of wood and leaves and earth and bodies. We had to stick to one of the tracks, moving along it at speed.

That was when the German shells started coming down. The first was 50 yards ahead of us. There was a huge plume of dust and smoke, a sharp reek of burning and then a silence. A ringing in the ears.

Next came the screams of pain and panic.

I looked to my right as we marched past the site where the shell had hit. It was covered in bodies. Some weren't moving. Others jerked around, mouths gaping open. Our orders were to leave them and advance, just as they would leave us. We heard them calling out for help. Screaming in pain. But we had to move on.

There was no time to think about those men and their lives. We thought only of our purpose. To take the German positions.

Nothing else mattered.

The shelling had scattered our units. Now we had to slash through undergrowth, heading towards the German lines, away from the track and the shells.

I looked up and saw Fred Bullock just ahead of me, leading the way like he always did. I waved to my men to follow him. As we struggled through the undergrowth behind him, a memory came into my head. Fred at his front door with his three kids jumping on him.

Then, all of a sudden, men began coughing. Then there was a terrible fumbling for gas masks. I snatched at mine too, feeling horrific panic. Coughing in case I'd already inhaled gas.

But it wasn't gas. It was a dreadful smell, deep in this deadly wood. It was a stench that made it hard to breathe.

I soon saw the source of the smell. Under a canopy of trees, shaded from the July light, were dozens of bodies. Bodies black and swollen. Some were complete, some in pieces. Arms. Legs. Heads. All in British and South African uniforms. They'd been here for some time, long enough for the sun and heat to take their toll.

It's hard to imagine such a sight. Hard even to remember it.

But it was there. We saw it. Then we looked away.

That was when we saw the flies hanging like a great black shadow over the bodies.

"Come on," Bullock shouted as he led us to the left of the dead bodies. Always the captain, he snapped us out of this vile scene.

We were running now, through Delville Wood, our rifles out in front of us. The noise of the German machine guns had started up again and fragments of shattered trees were falling around us under the fire. Bullets whipped through the air. Some were going hundreds of yards too far, but others were hitting soldiers' bodies as they ran. There'd be a thumping sound, a cry of pain, then a man would hit the forest floor.

But we had to go on.

Then Bullock stopped. I picked up my pace to catch up with him and saw a pair of soldiers coming towards him. German soldiers. Their guns ahead of them, fixed with bayonets.

"Where the hell did they come from?" I shouted to Bullock.

He didn't turn round. Nor did he react to the sight of the Germans.

And then I understood why he had stopped. He was leaning against a tree. Still.

He'd been shot.

Of course. He'd been shot.

And now the two Germans were moving towards him to finish him off.

In war, there are moments when all the noise and smells and tastes fade. Everything goes still. The machine guns stop firing. There are moments when it is just you and what you have to do to survive.

I ran hard down the hill, desperate to reach Bullock before the Germans did, keeping the tree between me and them to cover my approach.

I took the first German by surprise as I came from behind the tree. I drove my bayonet into his chest, feeling the crunching of his bones as I did so, then drawing it back to drive it into his throat

as a second German came at me. And, somehow, I found strength I'd never used before, strength that seemed to rip the muscles from my bones. I lifted the first German into the path of the second and he rammed his bayonet into his comrade, giving me time to remove my bayonet from the first German's body, pull it back and fire a bullet into the second German's head. He fell back, his gun still stuck in his comrade's back, his face in pieces.

I did this like I was a machine. I used the skills I'd learned on bags of straw at Holmbury Park. It was easy. It was like a training drill in football. A set of movements. I felt nothing.

TWENTY-FOUR

After Delville Wood, we had the final of the Flanders Cup. A day to be a footballer, not a soldier. To warm up, I stretched muscles that nights in the trenches had made bunched and stubborn.

My mind was bunched and stubborn too.

The players and the crowd knew that the whole battalion was going back to the front-line trenches the next day. And everyone knew that there was another big push coming. Men would be sent over the top. Men would be mown down by machine-gun fire. Men would be gassed and blown apart by stick bombs, hand grenades and shells. We all knew that.

Who knows how they had got there, but there were sports reporters at the match from London

newspapers. Whatever happened today would be big news back home.

Sid Wheelhouse and Fred Bullock urged me on. They wanted to win this with a clean sheet. Then we'd have made it through the whole tournament without giving away a goal. That was worth fighting for. But Bullock looked like less of a barn door that day, still in bandages two or three weeks after Delville Wood.

He was lucky to be alive. We all were.

The pitch wasn't as muddy as it had been against the Essex and Staffordshire battalions, so the Footballers passed the ball well. Our opponents were hardly able to keep up with us. We were professional footballers, after all. Professional soldiers too. We won.

We overwhelmed the Kings Rifles. 11–0.

After the final whistle, Brigadier-General Daly handed us each a medal. A proper Cup Final medal, minted in the same forge as the FA Cup Final medals. Then he handed the trophy to Major Buckley, who refused it and insisted it went to Bullock, then Wheelhouse, then me. The crowd cheered, and then headed off as rain came sweeping across the Somme.

Wheelhouse and Bullock were thrilled. They'd defended their goal perfectly all tournament.

"Have you ever scored eight goals in a game before?" Wheelhouse asked me.

"Never," I said.

The next arm around me was Major Buckley's. He congratulated me on my performance, then told me again, in a low voice, that he would build a team around me back in Britain. A team that would win trophies. After the war.

TWENTY-FIVE

After our victory in the Flanders Cup, the soldiers of the Footballers' Battalion faced weeks of war. Sometimes we were away from the front line, but there was no real relief in that. It was like coming up for air when you were drowning, then being pushed back under again. All we did then was sleep and eat. There was no football.

In every battle, we lost men to terrible deaths. I felt it was only a matter of time before I faced the same terrible death myself.

But there were some mercies.

Bullock's flesh wound had healed.

Summers was well too. He wrote to tell me he was living in some country house near Huddersfield, which made me smile.

Wheelhouse, Bailey and Buckley had made it as far as I had. They were alive. That was as much as we could hope for.

I was mentioned in dispatches after Delville. For risking my own life to rescue Bullock. But there were dozens of others I didn't rescue in that wood.

Summer passed. Autumn was coming. The temperatures were dropping at night. Soon the first frosts would bite. Then snow. And hail. Another winter in the trenches.

Until then we had to cope with the rain. We had our waterproofs, but rain still found its way into our hair, our necks, down our backs, into our boots. Everything we owned or wore, everything that should have been dry, was wet.

The rain was the Germans' ally. For two nights they'd been sending over hundreds of mortars, aiming for our lines with more and more success.

Men were dying.

Trenches were collapsing, the parapets sliding in on us. Everything was buried in thick, oozing mud. And, without a parapet, it was hard to shoot and not be shot at. Hard to attack and not be attacked.

We needed to rebuild the parapets to make the trenches good again.

A party of 12 men was sent out. It was cold and wet and dark. Mawson was one member of the party. Wheelhouse another.

I had volunteered, but I wasn't among them this time.

They went out with their digging tools in the dark. They were soaked, muddy and exhausted, even before

the work began. Perhaps the scraping of their tools alerted the Germans to their activity. Or maybe a sentry scanned No Man's Land when the flares were up. Day or night, it was dangerous to be outside the trenches.

The blast was all the louder because of the quiet that came before it.

I had been watching through a collapsed loophole. I covered my eyes to avoid the worst of the flash. Then I looked again. I needed to report back. Had they been hit?

At first I thought the answer was no. They were all still there. I could see their black shapes dripping mud and rain. I was about to shout back to my captain, when I saw them grabbing at their sides.

All at once.

For their packs.

There was no mistaking their fumbling and snatching.

"GAS!" I yelled, as loud as I could. "GAS! GAS!"

Then I put on my own gas mask and looked round to make sure everyone had heard me. The bell was ringing now as we stood, black-faced, peering at each other through tiny panes of glass. There was a sickening smell of rubber and of fear.

Then they came over the top. Our dozen men slid down the ruined muddy trenches, away from the gas.

They were chased by a slow-moving cloud that seemed to pour itself over the landscape. Mawson came first. Then three more. Then Wheelhouse. None of them with their gas masks on.

Coughing.

Grimacing.

Vomiting.

I knew it was bad – really bad.

Each of us in the trench grabbed a mud-covered man and helped him put his gas mask on. And all the while, the gas flowed silently into our trench.

These men had had a lungful.

They were doomed and we knew it just as well as they did. They were going to die.

Some had already stopped breathing. Mawson was dead. Others wheezed. Their eyes rolled, they frothed at the mouth, and their faces turned purple.

I went with Wheelhouse. He seemed less affected by the gas. He kept saying he was all right. But I took him to the field hospital all the same.

I walked behind him, carrying his rifle and my rifle. I had his gas mask too, now the threat had gone. He was breathing heavily, stumbling and coughing, but he insisted on walking without my

help. We waded through ankle-deep water in the trenches, mud sliding off the walls around us.

I had his back all the way, there for him if he needed me. I thought of when I'd first met him. At Leeds Road. At Huddersfield Town. This big, solid man who had stopped me getting at the Grimsby goal. It seemed a long time ago. So long that I wondered if it had really been us, or two completely different people.

As we walked, men moved out of Wheelhouse's way. I could tell from their faces that he looked rough. But he was walking, I told myself. And if he was walking, he'd be all right.

Neither of us spoke.

TWENTY-SIX

The field hospital was an old barn with a tarp over its caved-in roof. Rain hammered down on the canvas as I sat next to Wheelhouse.

Wheelhouse was lying on his side, his knees up to his chest. His skin was pale and moist. His cheeks were sunken like an old man's. He reeked of the vile gas that was now in his lungs.

Wheelhouse put his hand on mine.

"Jack," he asked. "Will you write a letter?"

"I will, Sid."

I'd never called him by his first name before. But then he had never called me by mine.

There was paper and a pencil on top of an upturned shell crate. I reached for them.

Sid took a breath. "Agnes Wheelhouse," he said slowly.

A breath.

"32 Neville Street."

Another breath.

"New Cleethorpes."

Breath.

"Lincs."

Then he had to rest. He wheezed in and out, out and in. Flecks of bloody foam came from his lips. I could see panic in his face. He was afraid he might not finish his letter. His vital letter.

That fear forced him to try again.

It took almost an hour for Sid to dictate his letter to his wife. He spoke in strings of two or three words.

144

"My dear

Agnes.

I hope

this letter finds

the family well.

It is

bad this time,

my love.

Do what

you must do

to care for

the children.

When Arthur is

fourteen,

please give him

my football medals.

I promised him them.

Do what you need

to do for

yourself.

Think only

of yourselves. Please

tell my

mother and father

that I

remembered them.

Tell them that I

love them.

Stand firm.

I am forever

at your

shoulder.

Your loving husband,

Sidney."

I dated the letter, 18th September 1916. Then I looked at him. Sid Wheelhouse. My friend. The footballer. His eyes were closed after the effort of speaking his letter.

He was breathing faster, his chest rising and falling. His face was darker. I took a cloth from a bowl of water, wrung it out, dabbed his forehead, put my hand on his.

His eyes would never open again. I knew that. I had seen this happen before. When he reared up and arched his back, I closed my eyes too, still holding his hand.

And when I opened my eyes, Sid Wheelhouse was gone.

I stared out at the grey rain clouds sweeping endlessly across the French fields, then I sealed Sid's letter and slipped it into my top pocket. I folded it inside the cartoon I kept. The one given

to me by Larrett Roebuck's widow in Huddersfield nearly two years before, on the day I first met Sid Wheelhouse.

PART 4
Footballer

TWENTY-SEVEN

It was 1919. The war was over.

Many of my friends were dead, but I had survived. I could go back to my old life.

Onto the pitch.

Over the line.

Every time I ran out as a footballer, I felt an explosion inside.

Since my return from the war, Brentford had won the London Combination League twice. I was their leading scorer. And now that professional football had begun again, I had returned to Huddersfield. But there were rumours of much bigger teams wanting me.

Sheffield United. Arsenal. Fulham.

Or perhaps I was being lined up for Norwich City. Major Buckley was the manager there – and I'd not forgotten his promise back in France that he'd build a team around me after the war.

It was all good on the pitch. I was happy on the pitch.

Off the pitch, it wasn't quite so good.

I couldn't close my eyes at night for fear of seeing flare bursts. I had taken to sitting in the cellar, to get away from the sky. Things could fall out of the sky. Even the cellar rats were better than the dark sky above me.

During the day, I had started to see people in London crowds. People I shouldn't be able to see. Dead people. Bradstreet, the lieutenant, was one. I saw him everywhere. It became a sad joke for me. I'd call out to him, then I'd be overcome by laughter. Of a sort.

My troubles weren't unusual. We were all a little unsteady after the war.

The oddest thing happened on a winter afternoon when I was playing on Griffin Park for Brentford.

I'd just scored my third goal. A hat-trick. The crowd was cheering. I looked up to give them a wave.

And then I saw him. His powerful body. His broad, honest face.

Sid Wheelhouse.

As clear as day.

I ran up to the edge of the stand and gestured to him. But he'd disappeared. I called to people in the crowd to tell Wheelhouse it was me, that he should stay, come and meet me after the game. We could go for a beer. Talk about the old days.

TWENTY-EIGHT

I was back in Huddersfield, playing professional football again, when Major Buckley called me one morning. He asked me to meet him in London on urgent business.

We met at a bar in Kings Cross station. Kings Cross had changed since I was last there. Its bricks and mortar were the same. But the people were different. There were people going about their business. Working people. Far fewer uniforms.

It seemed that London was getting back to normal. And there were some days – like today – when I was doing better too. Today I had something to get out for, something to drown out the noise of my memories.

Major Buckley had come by train from Norwich to meet me. He shook my hand and I held onto it to be sure he wasn't a ghost.

"You look good," he said. "You're fit. You're scoring goals."

We talked about our old friends in the trenches. That was what always happened when men from the trenches met up again. We'd talk about who was doing well, who was going mad, who was dead. And then we could move onto other topics.

Buckley filled me in on what he knew.

Jack Woodward was at Chelsea, helping to sign and train players.

Joe Bailey had fought to the very end of the war – and lived.

Percy Summers was playing for Luton. He was one of the most promising keepers in the country now.

"What about Bullock?" Buckley asked me. "Back in the heart of his family?"

"He's well," I said. "Getting on."

And then Buckley did the other thing that men from the trenches did when they met. They didn't pry. He could tell from my reply that Bullock was not all right. I didn't want to talk about how low my old friend and captain was, how he was only half the man he used to be. Fred Bullock kept on being a victim of the war long after peace was declared.

We had talked about everybody we needed to talk about. I expected him to offer me a place next.

"I don't want you at Norwich," Buckley said.

"What?"

I almost spat the word out. Perhaps I sounded angry. I had been so sure he was going to take me.

"You don't belong there," he said.

"But ..."

"But I said I'd build a team around you? I meant it," Buckley said. "But there's someone else who wants to talk to you first."

I narrowed my eyes. "Who?"

"Jack Woodward."

"Eh?"

"Do you know where he is now?" Buckley asked.

"Chelsea," I said. "You just told me that."

"That's right," Buckley said. "We can't afford you at Norwich. Chelsea will have to break the transfer record to bring you south."

TWENTY-NINE

I'd not been to Stamford Bridge since I was a fan watching Woodward score goal after goal for Chelsea.

Now I was waiting outside his office.

"Jack," he said. "Come in."

Jack? He had called me Jack. He had only ever called me "Private" or "Corporal". There was no way I could call him Jack.

Jack Woodward.

Chelsea and England.

My hero. Once upon a time.

"Hello, sir," I said.

"Please," Woodward said. "Call me Jack."

I looked down at his walking stick. "How is the leg, sir?" I asked.

"It'll be like this for ever," he said. "I've had to give up any idea of playing football. Serious football. But I can have other roles in the game. I'm working for Chelsea as a ... a scout of sorts," he said.

"Yes, sir," I said. "Major Buckley told me."

Then Woodward took me on a tour of the ground. After about an hour – with not a word about the war – we were back at his desk. He sat and studied me.

"We're very interested in bringing you to Chelsea, Jack." He said it so fast that I almost missed it.

"I'm on a contract with Huddersfield Town, sir," I said.

"Chelsea would be willing to pay Huddersfield Town a transfer fee."

I didn't know how to respond.

"Go back to Yorkshire," Woodward said. "We'll be in touch."

We shook hands. He gripped mine firmly.

As I walked out of the door, back into the noise of London, Woodward called my name.

"Jack," he said. "Did you hear that they fixed the date for the first full England fixture? Against Ireland in October?"

"I did, sir."

He smiled. "Well, good luck," he said.

"Thank you," I replied. "Sir."

I walked out, my mind on Woodward's words to me. What did he mean? Good luck for the transfer? Or something else?

Surely not.

I turned to watch him walk away with his stick and his war wound – England's former centre forward. My mind was flooded with questions.

What if?

What if I could play for Chelsea and England?

Was that dream too much to hope for?

OCTOBER 1919

Ireland v England at Windsor Park, Belfast

The war has been over for less than a year. And I
am going over the line. I am playing for my country.

The noise hits me as we come out onto the pitch
to the roar of thousands of Irishmen. It makes me
flinch. I suspect I'm not the only one. But this time,
the blast of noise doesn't make me miss my stride.

This is it.

This is the day I have dreamed about. This is
the dream that kept me going in the dark, under
fire, shells coming at me, flares over me, trenches
collapsing on me. The dream I used to block it
all from my mind. Woodward's shredded leg. Me,
crawling across the mud and into the crater in

No Man's Land, leaving Summers behind. Me, running at that German, forcing my bayonet into his chest and throat, killing him.

The national anthems play.

And now I can feel it. The will. The burning desire. The energy that has brought me to where I am. About to play for my country.

The referee places the ball on the centre spot. I line up with my fellow players. I am the first to touch the ball, kicking off the match. I knock the ball sideways to Carr, then head up field. This is what I did before the war. This is what I do now.

Carr plays the ball forward to Turnbull, who makes quick ground up the wing.

I have made quick ground too. I am in the penalty area and I am ready.

Turnbull sees me. He sends the ball across, trying to catch the Irish defence cold.

Which it does.

I time my run. The ball is coming over. High in the bright sky over Belfast.

I move towards a space between two defenders. They don't know how to stop me with the ball at my feet. I trap it with my right foot, then hit it hard with my left. I see it strike the underside of the bar, then bounce just over the line.

Goal.

No question. The referee points back to the centre circle.

Thirty seconds into the game, thirty seconds into my international career and I've scored a goal for England.

So many men are dead and gone and their dreams will never come true. But I am alive. I survived. And I owe it to them to live. To play. To win.

ABOUT *OVER THE LINE*

Over the Line is based on real events and real people, but it is a novel, not a history book.

I could not have written this novel on my own.

When a historian friend told me about Jack Cock's life and how he had scored England's first international goal after the end of the First World War, I wanted to help tell Jack's story.

I looked at photographs and documents about the real footballers, soldiers and battles described in this book. In 2011, I visited the Somme, and I went to Delville Wood. I found Sid Wheelhouse's grave beside a farmer's field. It was then that I understood very clearly that *Over the Line* needed to be accurate and sensitive to the real men who had fought in the trenches.

Tom Palmer

WHAT HAPPENED TO THE FOOTBALLERS AND SOLDIERS IN *OVER THE LINE* AFTER THE FIRST WORLD WAR?

FRANK BUCKLEY

Major Frank Buckley played a very important part in the Footballers' Battalion. He went on to be a leader after the war too – he managed some of the great teams of the English game, including Wolverhampton Wanderers and Leeds United. He was famous for trying out new tactics for training and playing, and for finding young players who would become huge stars. One such player was Billy Wright, a legend for Wolves and England. During his long career, Frank Buckley won every top flight competition in the English game.

FRED BULLOCK

Fred Bullock was the captain of Huddersfield Town and played for them over a period of eleven years, broken by the war. After he was injured at the Battle of the Somme,

he was treated in hospital in England. He went on to play 202 times for his club, and won one cap for England in 1920, before retiring to run a pub in Huddersfield. Fred Bullock died from ammonia poisoning when he was just 36.

JACK COCK

After he signed for Chelsea, Jack Cock scored 21 goals in 25 games in his first season. He later played for Plymouth, Everton and Millwall. Off the football pitch, Jack enjoyed a short career as an actor. He appeared in two films, *The Winning Goal* and *The Great Game*, as well as singing on the stage. Jack, like Fred, retired to run a pub in London.

PERCY SUMMERS

Percy Summers was one of Sid Wheelhouse's team-mates at Grimsby Town. As a goalkeeper, he began his career with several seasons at Chesterfield, his hometown team. Percy survived the war and went on to play for Luton and Margate.

SID WHEELHOUSE

When Sid died at the age of just 28, he left a wife and three children in Grimsby. Sid was as popular on the pitch as in the trenches, and on his death the *Athletic News* described him as "a fine man, clean living, high minded, chivalrous

and a model professional". He is buried at Couin Cemetery on the Somme. Tom Palmer visited Sid Wheelhouse's grave and, later, met members of his family, who said how proud they are that *Over the Line* tells Sid's story and will help children today understand what happened 100 years ago.

JACK WOODWARD

Vivian John "Jack" Woodward was England's leading goal scorer until 1958. Even now, he still has the best goals-per-game average for any established England player, with 29 goals in 23 appearances. Before the events described in *Over the Line*, Jack captained Great Britain to winning the team gold at two consecutive Olympic Games. But, after the war, Jack's injury meant he could never play top-flight competitive football again.

ARMISTICE
RUNNER
TWO LIVES CONNECTED BY MEMORY
TOM PALMER

978-1-78112-825-1

OVER
THE LINE
EVEN IN THE TRENCHES, FOOTBALL LIVES ON
TOM PALMER

978-1-78112-956-2

AFTER
THE WAR
FROM AUSCHWITZ TO AMBLESIDE
TOM PALMER

D-DAY
DOG
TOM PALMER

978-1-78112-948-7

978-1-78112-868-8